Best in Show for

ROTTEN RALPH

Written by Jack Gantos

Illustrated by Nicole Rubel

Farrar Straus Giroux

New York

For Anne and Mabel —J.G.

For my family —N.R.

Text copyright © 2005 by Jack Gantos
Illustrations copyright © 2005 by Nicole Rubel
All rights reserved
Distributed in Canada by Douglas & McIntyre Publishing Group
Color separations by Chroma Graphics PTE Ltd.
Printed and bound in the United States of America by Berryville Graphics
Designed by Nancy Goldenberg
First edition, 2005
1 3 5 7 9 10 8 6 4 2

www.fsgkidsbooks.com

Library of Congress Cataloging-in-Publication Data
Gantos, Jack.
    Best in show for Rotten Ralph / written by Jack Gantos ; illustrated
by Nicole Rubel.— 1st ed.
        p.   cm.
    Summary: Hoping to beat his cousin Percy in the cat show, Ralph
allows Sarah to help him spruce up his image and get in shape.
    ISBN-13: 978-0-374-36358-1
    ISBN-10: 0-374-36358-7
    [1. Cat shows—Fiction.   2. Contests—Fiction.   3. Cats—Fiction.
4. Self-perception—Fiction.]   I. Rubel, Nicole, ill.   II. Title.

PZ7.G15334Be 2005
[E]—dc22

                                                                    2004040359

The character of Rotten Ralph was originally created by
Jack Gantos and Nicole Rubel

Contents

Cat-Show Jitters · 7

Bird-Beak Blahs · 17

A Tale of Two Kitties · 29

I Gotta Be Me! · 39

Cat-Show Jitters

Rotten Ralph had been in the bathroom for hours.

What is he doing in there? wondered Sarah. She knocked on the bathroom door. "Ralph," she called, "please open the door."

But Ralph didn't answer. He was thinking about the cat show. Ralph didn't want to be beaten by his cousin Percy.

Ralph practiced his smile. I am one good-looking cat, he said to himself.

But when he looked in the mirror, he wasn't sure.

Sarah jiggled the doorknob. "Ralph! I asked you nicely to open the door."

Ralph still didn't listen. He worked on his muscle-cat poses.

I am one tough kitty, he said to himself.

But when he looked in the mirror, his muscles seemed mousy.

Finally, Sarah had waited long enough.

"Open up or else!" she threatened.

Rotten Ralph opened the door. He looked upset.

"What's wrong?" Sarah asked when she saw his sad face.

Ralph pointed to the cat-show announcement.

"That should be fun," said Sarah.

No, Ralph thought. That will not be fun.

Just then, Percy and a few of his
furry friends stopped by.

"Percy's Posse for Perfection will be
cheering for me at the cat show," Percy
said. "Would you like to join?"

Ralph didn't think so.

"You might as well," Percy continued, "because I'm going to kink your tail."

The posse began to practice their cheers in Ralph's front yard.

"Percy is a prince! Percy's in the know! Percy's the cat who's Best in Show!"

13

Ralph slammed the door and growled.

Sarah smiled. "Don't worry, Ralph," she said. "I know just what to do."

Ralph wondered what she meant.

Bird-Beak Blahs

Later that day, Sarah found Ralph spread out on the couch watching TV. He was eating a bag of fried bird beaks. He burped.

Sarah took a long look at him and shook her head. "It is so sad," she whispered to herself, "when a cat has gone to the dogs."

She snapped off the TV.

"If you want to be a winner, you have
to train like one," said Sarah. "The
judges do not like a flabby-catty."

In the distance, Ralph heard Percy's
Posse practicing another perfect cheer.
He covered his ears but could not

help imagining Percy's victory party.

Ralph howled. I've had enough of this, he thought. That cat needs to be put in his place.

Now Ralph was ready to get off the couch.

Ralph wanted to be a winner. And Sarah had a plan to whip Ralph into shape.

She started by making Ralph do push-ups and sit-ups. She made him jump rope.

The next day, she made him climb up trees, and down. She made him chase wind-up mice and butterflies.

This is awful, Ralph thought. But it got worse.

"A true champion must *look* like a winner," Sarah declared.

She gave Ralph a hot bath. His fur was dried and brushed. His nails were clipped. His whiskers were waxed. His tail was straightened. His ears were cleaned and his teeth were scrubbed.

"Your posture must be proper," said Sarah.

By the end of the week, Ralph could walk all the way around the house with a fishbowl balanced on his head.

Sarah was very impressed. "I think you are ready to strut your stuff."

A Tale of Two Kitties

On the day of the cat show, Ralph was assigned a spot on the judging platform right near Percy's.

When Ralph took his place, Percy's Posse held up their signs.

Percy smiled sweetly at Ralph. "You don't stand a chance," he said.

"You don't scare me," Ralph answered.

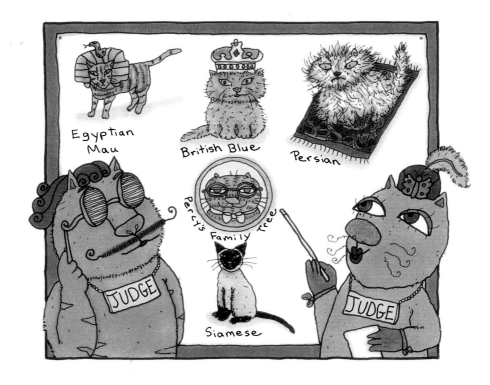

Soon the judges began to examine the cats. They looked at Percy's family tree.

"Very impressive," they all agreed.

They gave him high marks on their scorecards.

Then they looked at Ralph's family
tree.

"Oh dear," said one judge, "is he even
a cat?"

They gave him low marks.

"A perfect cat must have a perfect meow," said the judges.

Percy's croon brought the judges to tears.

Ralph's yowl made them hold their ears.

They gave him more low marks.

To show off his superior breeding, Percy recited a fancy poem.

"It is titled 'A Tale of Two Kitties,' " he began.

One was the best of kitties,
The other was the worst of kitties.
Only one kitty is Best in Show,
The other is the pest we all know.
For one kitty the cream rises to the top,
For that other one it sinks like a rock.
You must agree I am far ahead,
And the cat in red should have stayed in bed.

Ralph tried to think of a poem, but his mind went blank.

"What's wrong?" asked Percy. "Cat got your tongue?"

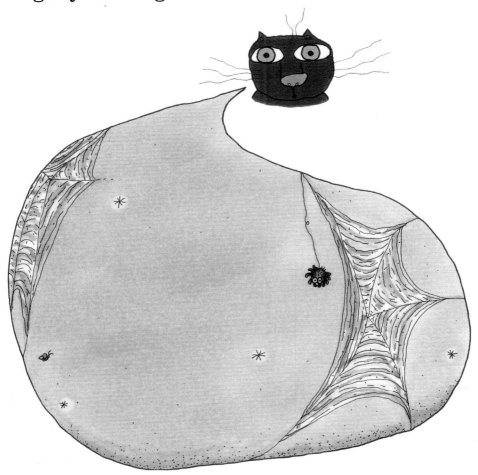

At intermission, when the judges were not looking, Ralph peeked at their scorecards.

Percy was ahead in everything. Ralph felt like giving up.

But Sarah was there to help. "Don't worry, Ralph," she said. "Just be yourself."

That was the kind of advice Ralph understood.

Being *me* is what I do best, he thought. He wasn't finished yet.

I Gotta Be Me!

At last, the judges called the cats back to the judging platform.

"It's time to show us your special cat skills and hobbies," they instructed.

Ralph smiled. My special skill is being rotten, he thought. I should stick to it.

When Percy displayed his flower-arranging finesse, Ralph displayed his karate moves.

After Percy demonstrated how to
make sushi, Ralph demonstrated how
to eat it.

Percy pulled a rabbit out of a hat.

Ralph made Percy disappear.

And while Percy performed a perfect
tap-dance routine . . .

. . . Rotten Ralph got the whole joint jumping.

Finally, the judges were ready to
make their decision. "Perfect Percy is
Best in Show," they said, and gave him
a perfectly tiny trophy.

"But," they declared, "Ralph is the
cat we want to know!" They gave him a
huge trophy for being "The Worst at
Being Best in Show."

"Oh, Ralph!" cried Sarah. "You might be the worst at being Best in Show, but you are the best at being yourself."

Ralph climbed into his trophy. "I love being me!" he purred.

05/06